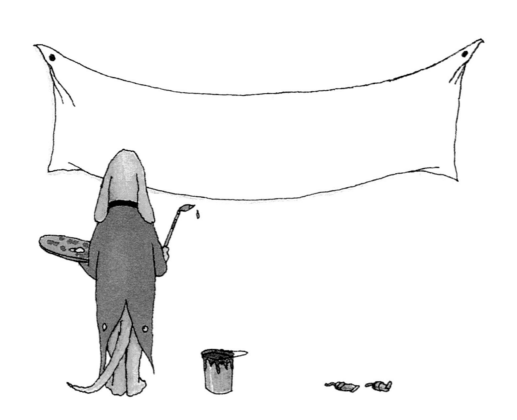

Aladdin Books

Macmillan Publishing Company   New York
Collier Macmillan Publishers   London

Story and Pictures by John Stadler

ALADDIN BOOKS
Macmillan Publishing Company
866 Third Avenue, New York, NY 10022
Collier Macmillan Canada, Inc.

Animal Cafe is also published in a hardcover edition by Bradbury Press

First Aladdin Edition 1986

Printed in the United States of America

2 3 4 5 6 7 8 9 10

Library of Congress Cataloging-in-Publication Data
Stadler, John.
  Animal cafe.
  (Reading rainbow book)
  Summary: Old Max never suspects the true source of his shop's financial
success.
  [1. Restaurants, lunch rooms, etc.—Fiction.
2. Animals—Fiction]   I. Title. II. Series.
[PZ7.S77575An 1986]   [E]   85-26789
ISBN 978-0-6897-1063-6

To Al Manso

Maxwell owned a food shop. Sometimes business was good and sometimes business was bad.

But good or bad, it was all the same to Maxwell, for one morning each week he found that the foods on his shelves had vanished overnight and his cash register was stuffed full of money.

"Must be magic," he said.

As Maxwell closed the shop one Friday evening, he said to his cat and dog:

"You, Casey, you're such a lazy cat you couldn't catch a mouse if it were sitting on top of your nose. And you, Sedgewick, some watchdog you are! A burglar with bells on his feet wouldn't keep you from snoring. Sleep! Sleep! Sleep! All you do is sleep."

"Sweet dreams," Maxwell whispered as he left the shop.

In a flash Sedgewick and Casey were up and about. "All clear!" Sedgewick called from the doorway.

Casey was already in the kitchen slicing, dicing and spicing.

"What are you cooking tonight?" Sedgewick asked. "I'm writing out the menus."

"It's an old family recipe – a tasty dish of chipped beef with a touch of cheddar cheese, some chopped liver and lima beans, with some spinach, garlic and prune juice tossed in for good measure."

"Fine. We'd better call it Casey's Combustible Casserole," Sedgewick said.

Then Sedgewick ran from place to place decorating the shop.

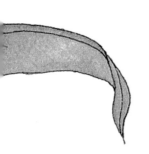

From outside Casey and Sedgewick heard the sound of approaching footsteps and chattering voices. Someone pounded on the door.

"Just in time," Casey cheered.

"Welcome back, friends," Sedgewick said as he opened the door to the first guests.

"Delighted, I'm sure," answered Mrs. O'Hare.

"Wouldn't miss it for the world," added her husband.

"Uh, oh!" Casey whispered. "Here comes Cutlet! Last time he ate us out of house and home. And then he complained about the meal being pork 'n' beans."

"Just be nice," Sedgewick said through a stiff smile. "Well, *hello* Cutlet. We were just talking about you. Welcome."

"Welcome, schmelcome," Cutlet snorted. "Where's the food?"

Soon many more guests arrived.

Professor Tuskanini of Huxley College was there, as well as Dr. Quackk. Lady Dumont was not far behind, accompanied by Colonel Kangaroo (retired).

All the guests mingled happily, discussing this and that.

"This," said one.

"That," said another.

Sedgewick saw that it was growing late and hurried the guests to their tables.

"What do you think of it?" Sedgewick asked after he served Casey's Combustible Casserole.

"It's – uh – well – I would say – er – undoubtedly it's – uh . . ." replied Miss Goose.

The guests ate lightly, except for Cutlet who constantly cried out for more.

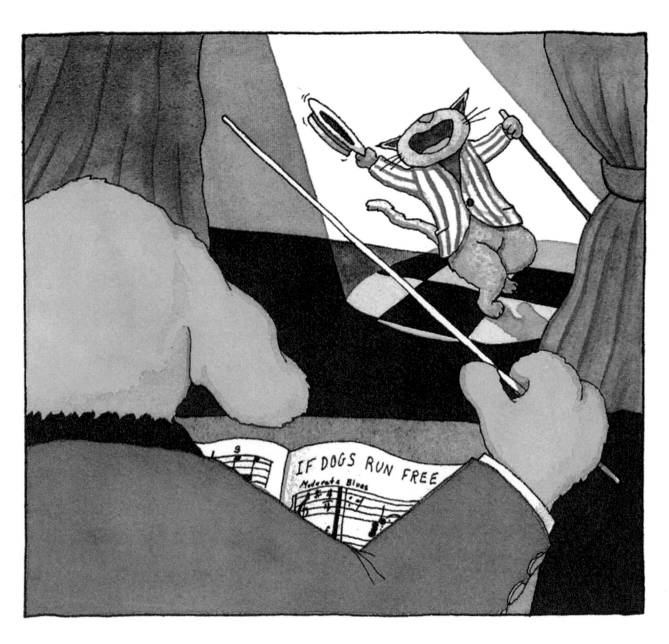

IF DOGS RUN FREE

Moderate Blues

After dinner Sedgewick and Casey started the entertainment. First Casey juggled, and then he sang and danced. Then Sedgewick told jokes as Casey performed daredevil stunts. Finally they sang some old favorites together.

"Bravo!" roared Hubert the Bear.

"Mais oui!" cried Alicia La Gator as she got up to dance.

Suddenly Casey looked at the clock. "Yikes!" he
yelled. "It's almost dawn. Maxwell will be back soon."
The guests quickly lined up to pay their bills.
"Wonderful, wonderful," Lawrence Elk sang out.
"Oh, no," Casey shrieked as the last of the guests
filed out. "Look!"

Cutlet was lying on the floor groaning.
"He's eaten too much again," Sedgewick
complained. "We'll have to roll him out."

It was an enormous struggle.

Then Sedgewick and Casey rushed about to clean up the shop.

"Hurry," they yelled at each other, running in all directions at once. "Maxwell will be here any minute."

"I'm pooped," Casey whined as he scrubbed the dishes.

Sedgewick swept past him moaning, "Keep at it! He's coming..."

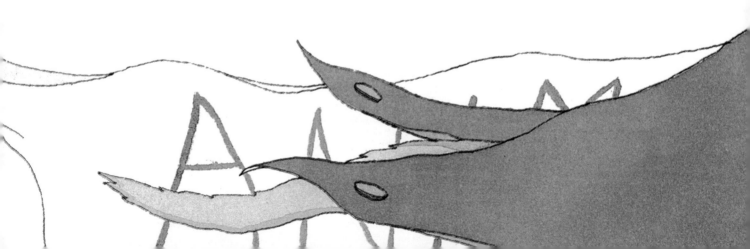

In a flash they finished the kitchen, washed up the shop, turned down the lights and locked all the money in the cash register. Just as Maxwell reached the door, Sedgewick and Casey dashed to the back of the shop, falling on top of each other in a heap.

Maxwell came in and turned on the lights. He opened the cash register and saw that it was full once again. And sure enough, his shelves were nearly bare.

"Must be magic!" he said.

Then he looked over at Sedgewick and Casey.

"Silly animals," he said. "All you ever do is sleep."

And that they did.

Made in the USA
San Bernardino, CA
26 August 2019